W9-CAR-305

FIREMAN SMALL
Fire Down Below!

Written and illustrated by **Wong Herbert Yee**

Houghton Mifflin Company
Boston 2001

www.houghtonmifflinbooks.com

The text of this book is set in 15-point Rockwell.
The illustrations are watercolor, reproduced in full color.

Library of Congress Cataloging-in-Publication Data

Yee, Wong Herbert.
Fireman Small—fire down below! / Wong Herbert Yee.
p. cm.
Summary: Having gone to the Pink Hotel to get some sleep,
Fireman Small detects a fire there and saves its animal guests.
ISBN 0-618-00707-5
[1. Firefighters—Fiction. 2. Hotels, motels, etc.—Fiction.
3. Animals—Fiction. 4. Stories in rhyme.] I. Title.
PZ8.3.Y42 Fif 2001
[E]—dc21
00-033481

Printed in Singapore
TWP 10 9 8 7 6 5 4 3 2 1

For all firefighters,
big and small

In the middle of town, where buildings stand tall
There lives a little man called Fireman Small.
The only fireman this side of the bay
Is hungry and beat from working all day.

Outside the station, rain keeps pouring.
While Fireman Small sleeps, quietly snoring.

Plinkety-*plop,* a raindrop falls—
SPLAT!—on the nose of Fireman Small.
Over his bed, where the paint is peeling,
Rain trickles through a hole in the ceiling.

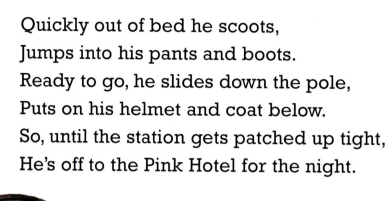

Quickly out of bed he scoots,
Jumps into his pants and boots.
Ready to go, he slides down the pole,
Puts on his helmet and coat below.
So, until the station gets patched up tight,
He's off to the Pink Hotel for the night.

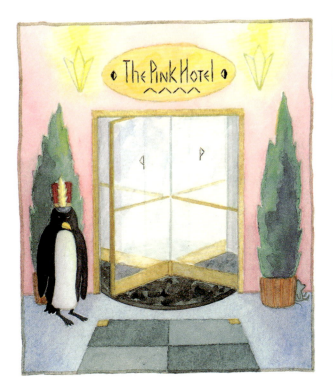

Fireman Small hangs a sign on the door:
Do NOT Disturb!—Room 224.
He closes the curtains, gets in bed,
And pulls the covers over his head.

Elevators creak riding up and down,
As folks prepare for a night on the town.
Doors slamming shut, hotel guests rushing,
Across the hall a toilet keeps flushing.

Outside, horns are honking: BEEP BEEP BEEP!
Too much noise for this fireman to sleep.
He finds cotton balls to plug up his ears,
And tosses and turns until traffic clears.
Just at the moment his droopy eyes close,
Something disturbing starts tickling his nose.

Quickly out of bed he scoots,
Jumps into his pants and boots.

What could be making that *terrible* smell?
Oh NO! There's a *fire* at the Pink Hotel!
Grabbing a towel to wrap round his arm,
He smashes the case to sound the alarm.

Pounding on doors to let everyone know,
"Hurry—HURRY! Fire down below!"
Miss Hippo is singing, "Rub-a-dub-dub."
She hears the alarm but gets stuck in the tub!

Out on a ledge Possum's ready to leap.
Mother Hen's chicks are crying: peep peep peep!

Fireman Small shouts to Alligator,
"No, no, NO, not the elevator!
Up, up, UP the stairwell you go.
Hurry—HURRY! Fire down below!"

Smoke-filled halls make it harder to see.
Farmer Pig thinks it's just the TV.
Fireman Small cries, "It's not the show!
Hurry—HURRY! Fire down below!"

"There's no time to dress or make up the bed,
Just grab a wet towel to cover your head."

Toad's in a tizzy, hopping and croaking.
The jazz band next door is really smoking.
"Your poncho's on fire!" wails drummer Mole.
Fireman Small hollers, "Stop—drop—and roll!"

"Up, up, UP the stairwell you go.
Hurry—HURRY! Fire down below!"

Trapped on the roof, they shiver and huddle,
Drenched to the bone, knee-deep in a puddle.
Fireman Small searches, splashing around.
A way off this building *has* to be found.

A *flash* of lightning! A thunder—CLAP!
Reveals the only way out of this trap.

The fire escape leads to the alley below!
Quickly down the steps hotel guests go.

For Fireman Small, there's no time to relax.
He grabs hold of his tiny fire ax.
Without hook and ladder or fire hose,
Back up the fire escape he goes.

WHACK! WHACK! WHACK!
His ax whirls in the air.

WHACK! WHACK! WHACK!
A hole here! A hole there!

The Pink Hotel's roof turns into a drain.
Down, down, down swirls the pouring rain.
It rushes and gushes from floor to floor—

WHOOSH! — past the lobby and out the front door.

Employees and guests are prancing about,
Singing, "HIP HIP HOORAY! The fire is out!"

But where will the guests spend their vacation?

There's still lots of room at the fire station.